P9-DNM-104

The Day
Jake
Vacuumed

WITHDRAWN
LVC BISHOP LIBRARY

LEBANON VALLEY COLLEGE LIBRARY

Timmy the cat

This Jake book
belongs to

. . . .

To Tricia, Mike, Yasmin, and Natasha
— with love

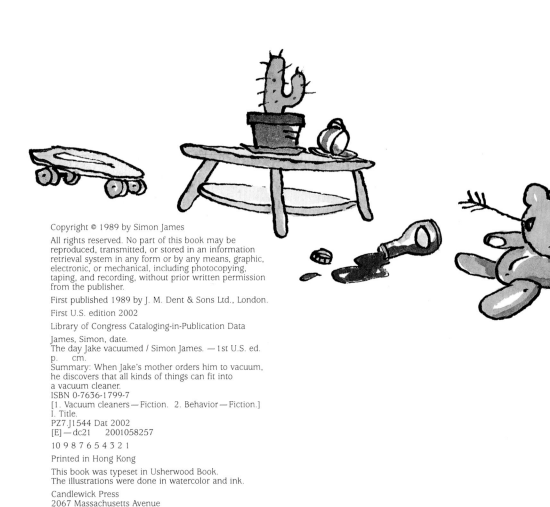

Copyright © 1989 by Simon James

All rights reserved. No part of this book may be reproduced, transmitted, or stored in an information retrieval system in any form or by any means, graphic, electronic, or mechanical, including photocopying, taping, and recording, without prior written permission from the publisher.

First published 1989 by J. M. Dent & Sons Ltd., London.

First U.S. edition 2002

Library of Congress Cataloging-in-Publication Data

James, Simon, date.
The day Jake vacuumed / Simon James. — 1st U.S. ed.
p.   cm.
Summary: When Jake's mother orders him to vacuum, he discovers that all kinds of things can fit into a vacuum cleaner.
ISBN 0-7636-1799-7
[1. Vacuum cleaners — Fiction. 2. Behavior — Fiction.]
I. Title.
PZ7.J1544 Dat 2002
[E] — dc21   2001058257

10 9 8 7 6 5 4 3 2 1

Printed in Hong Kong

This book was typeset in Usherwood Book.
The illustrations were done in watercolor and ink.

Candlewick Press
2067 Massachusetts Avenue
Cambridge, Massachusetts 02140

visit us at www.candlewick.com

The Day Jake Vacuumed

Simon James

CANDLEWICK PRESS
CAMBRIDGE, MASSACHUSETTS

Jake was difficult.
Jake was a problem.
He didn't like doing
anything for anyone.

So you can imagine how Jake felt when one day his mother asked him to do the vacuum cleaning.
For a while, Jake played with the machine, enjoying the loud noise it made.

Then a really wicked idea occurred to him.
Very quietly he crept over to Timmy, the cat.
Aiming the nozzle at Timmy, Jake switched on
the vacuum cleaner and sucked up the poor cat!
Jake was delighted.

Jake knew he would be in trouble.
"I might as well make it
BIG TROUBLE!" thought Jake.
He sneaked off to the kitchen . . .

. . . and he sucked his mother up into the vacuum cleaner, rubber gloves and all!

"Yippee. I'm free!" shouted Jake.
"No one to tell me to do anything!"
He had the whole house to himself,
except that is, for his sister upstairs.

Jake's sister was in her bedroom,
playing with her dolls.
In crept Jake.
He climbed on top of the closet
and switched on the vacuum cleaner.
You can imagine what happened then.

But, oh dear! Jake remembered
that his father would be home soon.
There was only one thing to do.

At six o'clock on the dot, Jake's father opened
the front door. Out jumped Jake with the
vacuum cleaner roaring on full power.
It was a difficult fit at first, but eventually . . .
POP! In went Jake's father.
"Hooray!" shouted Jake.

Jake was delighted.
At last he was in charge!
He was so pleased that he decided to
suck up the WHOLE room, and indeed,
the whole page of this book . . .

. . . leaving only himself and the vacuum cleaner. Jake was free.

But Jake hadn't noticed that the vacuum
cleaner was now stuffed to the bursting
point and about to explode.

And explode it did, with a gigantic bang!
Once Jake's parents had recovered, they were furious.
They sent him to bed early—without any supper.

But Jake didn't mind. At least he knew he would never ever be asked to do the vacuuming again.

love from
Jake

LEBANON VALLEY COLLEGE LIBRARY

Simon James is the author-illustrator of many acclaimed books for children, including *The Day Jake Vacuumed, Jake and the Babysitter, Jake and His Cousin Sidney, Days Like This, The Wild Woods,* and *Leon and Bob,* which was named a *New York Times Book Review* Best Illustrated Children's Book of the Year.

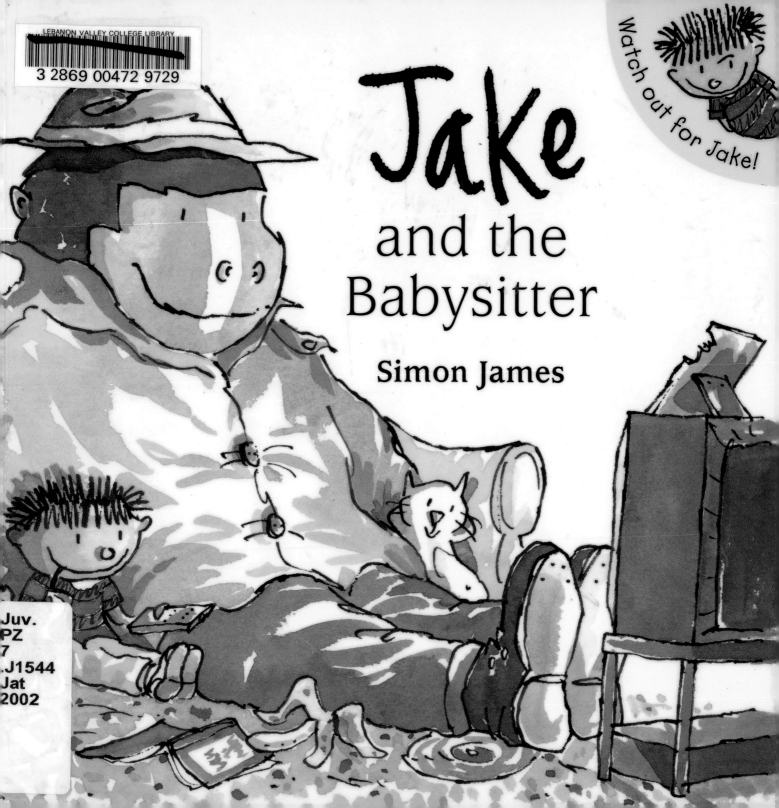

Jake
and the
Babysitter

Simon James

LEBANON VALLEY COLLEGE LIBRARY

3 2869 00472 9729

Juv.
PZ
7
.J1544
Jat
2002

Watch out for Jake!

Collect all three outrageous books about naughty Jake!

JAKE AND THE BABYSITTER

He's huge, he's hairy, and he's like no other babysitter Jake has ever had! Will Jake get in trouble again, or is his babysitter equally interested in monkeying around?

Paperback ISBN 0-7636-1800-4

JAKE AND HIS COUSIN SIDNEY

The only idea more horrifying than babysitting Jake is Jake babysitting a real live baby! Can he stay out of trouble while taking care of his cousin Sidney?

Paperback ISBN 0-7636-1801-2

THE DAY JAKE VACUUMED

When Jake's mother asks him to vacuum, he is determined to be as wicked as he can. Will anything (or anyone) avoid Jake and the vacuum?

Paperback ISBN 0-7636-1799-7

EAN

ISBN 0-7636-1800-4

9 780763 618001

50499